Barbie
THE Princess & THE Popstar

A Panorama Sticker Storybook

Based on the screenplay by Elise Allen
Adapted by Jill L. Rosenblum
Illustrated by Ulkutay Design Group

Special thanks to: Sarah Buzby, Cindy Ledermann, Ann McNeill, Dana Koplik, Emily Kelly,
Sharon Woloszyk, Tanya Mann, Julia Phelps, Carla Alford, Rita Lichtwardt, Kathy Berry, Rob Hudnut, David Wiebe,
Shelley Dvi-Vardhna, Michelle Cogan, Gabrielle Miles, Rainmaker Entertainment, and Walter P. Martishius.

Reader's Digest
Children's Books®

New York, New York • Montréal, Québec • Bath, United Kingdom

Meribella was buzzing with excitement. Its week-long 500th birthday celebration was beginning. Princess Tori was dutifully greeting a long line of guests at the royal reception, while the pop star, Keira, was performing in Meribella's amphitheater.

Even though Tori was a beautiful princess, she was tired of all her royal responsibilities. She longed to be at Keira's rock concert having fun.

Keira, too, wanted a break from her obligations. Although the concert was a huge hit and she was smiling for her fans, she was glad to finally close the door to her dressing room, grateful to escape the pressures of being a star.

Later that night, Tori was happy to be back in her bedroom where she didn't have to behave like a proper princess. "I wish I had her life," she said to her puppy, Vanessa, while looking up at the rocked-out Keira poster on her wall. She began to sing about what it would be like to be Keira.

Meanwhile, in her dressing room, Keira was looking at a portrait of the royal family. "Now there's a gig," she said to her playful bulldog, Riff. "Living in a castle, everything done for you—the princess probably never worked a day in her life."

Keira started to sing about what it would be like to be Princess Tori.

The next day, Keira and her power-hungry manager Crider, met the royal family at the castle. Princess Tori was thrilled to meet her favorite rock star as much as Keira was excited to meet a real princess.

"Wow! You've got more of *my* stuff than I do," Keira said looking at all the Keira posters in the princess's bedroom!

"You're a star!" said Tori in complete admiration of her new friend.

"And you're a princess!" said Keira. "I always dreamed of being one." Tori placed her tiara on Keira's head. Then Keira completed the transformation by using her magical microphone to turn her rocker outfit into a princess gown. Tori used her magical hairbrush and turned her princess hair into Keira's purple rocker do!

The girls had lots of fun with their magical transformations. Princess Tori now looked exactly like Keira and Keira had become Princess Tori!

The girls walked out of Tori's bedroom posing as each other.
"Can you keep a secret?" Tori asked Keira as they
stopped by a wall lined with photos of royal ancestors.
"Sure," replied Keira.
Tori rotated a carved flower on the wall. Suddenly,
the panel opened and they entered a beautiful
secret garden. In the center, a gardenia plant glittered
with almond-sized diamonds, and tiny garden fairies
were flying about taking care of all the plants.

"This plant is the Diamond Gardenia. It's 500 years old and it grows real diamonds! Legend says that the roots spread all through the kingdom. Without it, Meribella would wither and die," Tori explained.

Keira was amazed by the magic of the garden. Then, two Garden Fairies placed a diamond necklace on each girl. "We'll wear these as friendship necklaces," said Tori.

Meanwhile, Crider had secretly followed the girls into the garden. Diamonds glittered in his evil eyes as he planned to return to the garden when no one was watching to steal the valuable plant.

The girls had enjoyed being each other so much that they decided to continue their charade for another day. The next morning, the girls gave each other their daily schedules and advice on how to behave. They even traded dogs for the day!

"Ready?" asked Tori, decked out in her rocker outfit.

"Ready," said Keira, looking like the beautiful princess.

With Riff's help, Tori enjoyed her day as Keira. She managed the dance moves at rehearsal, gave out autographs, posed for the paparazzi, and loved trying on different costumes for the concert!

Likewise, Keira was getting used to the idea of being a princess. With Vanessa's guidance, she used the proper utensils at breakfast, judged a flower show, christened a yacht, and lunched with ambassadors. She even loved riding in the royal carriage waving to the people of Meribella!

Later that day, Keira and Tori shared the exciting details of being each other.

"This has been the best day I've had in like forever. Too bad the switch is over. Unless...you'd want to keep it going one more day...?" suggested Keira.

"You're on!" Tori said excitedly.

"But we have to switch back tomorrow before the live broadcast of my concert," said Keira.

The next day **everything** went wrong. Tori couldn't follow the footwork to Keira's dance and Keira managed to insult a visiting Duke! To make it even worse, Tori's Aunt Amelia had locked the princess in the bedroom for being improper at the table, and now she couldn't escape to meet Tori at the amphitheater!

Meanwhile, Tori was a nervous wreck. Keira was to perform on stage in ten minutes and she was nowhere in sight for the girls to switch back in time!

Tori was horrified to sing and dance in front of an audience, but she stepped out of Keira's dressing room ready for the opening number so that she wouldn't ruin her friend's career by not performing.

Trapped in the princess's bedroom, Keira watched Vanessa scratch at a wall, barking. Confused, Keira pushed on the wall, opening it to reveal a secret tunnel where she was able to escape!

Suddenly, the lights started to flicker throughout Meribella. Crider and his assistant had made their way into the secret garden and cut the roots of the Gardenia—causing the kingdom to completely wither! As the lights dimmed in the amphitheater, Tori knew something was wrong. She called an intermission and ran off stage.

Turning herself back into the real princess, Tori sped off to the castle in the royal carriage where she arrived just in time to help Keira chase away the thieves.

The girls rushed back to the secret garden to replant the gardenia, but it was too late, the plant was already dead.

Suddenly, the girls' faces lit up. "The friendship necklaces!" they gasped.

The girls quickly planted their diamonds as gardenia seeds and the Garden Fairies watered them. Magically, the seeds sprouted a tiny glittering gardenia plant with two shoots!

All of a sudden the kingdom came back to life. Keira and Tori raced back to the amphitheater just in time to finish the live concert where the audience was chanting Keira's name.

"I think this last song would sound great as a duet," said Keira. "Please welcome my best friend—her Royal Highness, Princess Tori."

As the crowd gave a thunderous applause, Keira and Tori smiled. They were happy that they had the chance to be each other, but they learned that the best thing they could be is themselves.

©Mattel

©Mattel

©Mattel

©Mattel